W9-CEC-558

THE NUTCRACKER

Retold by
Ronald Kidd

Illustrated by
Rick Reinert

Based on the tale
"The Nutcracker and the Mouse King"
by E. T. A. Hoffmann
and
"The Nutcracker Ballet"
by Peter Ilyich Tschaikovsky

Ideals Publishing Corp.
Nashville, Tennessee

Copyright © MCMLXXXV by Ideals Publishing Corporation
All rights reserved. Printed and Bound in U.S.A.
Published simultaneously in Canada.
ISBN 0-8249-8095-6

It was Christmas Eve, and in a small German village, snowflakes were falling. They drifted soundlessly from the sky, past chimneys and trees, settling to the ground in a thick white blanket.

The streets of the village were silent. But inside the Stahlbaum house there was warmth and light and laughter, for Dr. Stahlbaum and his family were giving a party.

Twelve-year-old Clara Stahlbaum knelt next to a door in the parlor, peeking through the keyhole into the drawing room. Her brother Fritz crouched next to her, and behind him stood eight other children.

"What do you see?" said Fritz.

"Nothing yet," she replied. "The grownups are just dancing and talking."

"Why can't we go in?" asked one of the younger children.

"It's a rule," said Fritz. "Children aren't allowed in the drawing room until the tree is lit."

"Here comes Father!" Clara exclaimed, jumping to her feet and shooing everyone back.

A moment later the door swung open, and the parlor was flooded with light. Dr. Stahlbaum stood there, beaming. "Merry Christmas, children!" he said.

They raced past him into the drawing room, with Fritz leading the way and Clara following close behind. Before them loomed a Christmas tree at least ten feet tall. But it wasn't the tree they were looking at. It was what lay beneath: presents.

There were sugar plums, bon-bons, toy soldiers, miniature swords and cannons, ceramic dolls, silk dresses, wooden horses, picture books, and dozens of other gifts. The children scurried about the tree, discovering treasure after treasure.

Then suddenly, in the midst of the gaiety, the front door burst open, and a cold breeze blew through the room. Everyone stopped for a moment, gazing toward the door and the darkness that lay beyond.

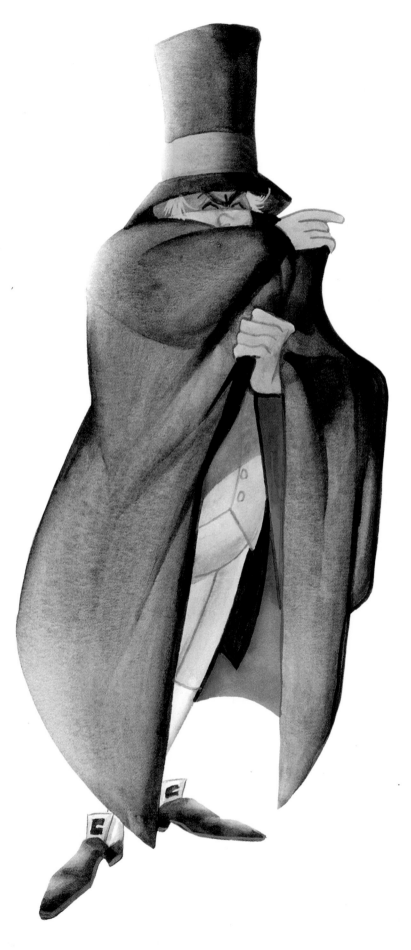

Out of the winter night stepped a man dressed in black. A tall hat covered his head, and he held a cape over his face, hiding everything but his eyes. The guests grew silent. Clara moved to her father's side and took his hand.

The man strode up to the group, the click of his boots echoing off the marble floor. Then he stopped and slowly drew aside the cape.

Behind it was the smiling face of Godpapa Drosselmeier. Besides being Clara's godfather, he was known throughout the village as a fixer of clocks and a master wood carver and inventor.

"Godpapa," said Clara, "you scared us."

Clara's godfather gave her a big hug. "My dear," he said, "I've brought you and the other children a surprise."

He removed his hat with a flourish, then motioned to a helper, who rolled out a large wooden puppet theater. As the children and their parents gathered around, Godpapa Drosselmeier climbed up behind the theater and took hold of the puppet strings.

The curtain opened to reveal a prince and princess dressed in white. As they walked together across the stage, a third puppet entered. It was a wicked-looking mouse, wearing a jeweled crown and carrying a sword. The mouse challenged the prince, who drew a sword of his own, and a fight began. With the children shouting encouragement, the prince held off his attacker. Then he moved forward. A moment later, the mouse lay at his feet.

The prince put away his sword and went to the princess. Kneeling, he kissed her hand. As he did, it seemed to Clara that the puppet strings and wooden stage and party guests melted away, leaving only the prince and princess in a land beyond care and time. It even seemed, for the briefest of moments, that Clara could feel the soft touch of the prince's kiss on the back of her own hand.

When Clara looked up, her godfather was standing over her, smiling. "I have more surprises," he
said. "Watch."

He drew the sides of his cape together in a great
circle, and when he opened them again, three
wooden figures stood on the floor in front of him: a
ballerina, a clown, and a Sugar Plum Fairy. To everyone's amazement, the figures began to move.

The ballerina pointed her toes and did an awkward pirouette. The clown did a series of stiff somersaults, wearing a pointed hat and a funny red nose. The Sugar Plum Fairy, lifting her delicate wings, flitted daintily about the room.

When the mechanical figures stopped moving, the guests clapped and cheered. Godpapa Drosselmeier took a deep bow, then turned to Clara. "And now," he said, "I have one more surprise. It's a special gift for a very special girl."

He closed his cape once more, then drew it open. Standing in front of Clara was another wooden figure wearing a handsome military jacket, hat, and sword. Its face, though, was anything but handsome. It was painted red, blue, and green, and had enormous eyes and a wide, gaping mouth.

Something about the face filled Clara with tenderness. She picked up the wooden figure and cradled it in her arms.

"What is it?" asked one of the children looking on.

"It's a nutcracker," replied Clara's godfather. He took a walnut from his pocket and placed it in the mouth of the little man. The mouth closed, breaking the nut into two neat pieces.

"Let me do that!" said Fritz. He grabbed the nut-cracker and tried to pull it away from his sister. There was a loud crack, and the head broke off.

"You've ruined him!" Clara cried. She held her precious gift close and wept bitterly, certain it would never be the same.

"Now, now, my dear," said Godpapa Drosselmeier. He took the two parts of the wooden figure
and went behind the puppet theater for a few moments. When he came out, he handed the nutcracker back to Clara.

"There, you see?" he said. "It's as good as new."
And so it was.

The musicians began playing again. The adults drifted off to eat pastries and exchange Christmas greetings. The children returned to the tree to play with their presents. And in one corner of the room, Clara held her nutcracker tight and danced a slow, blissful waltz.

Several hours later, after the guests had left and the family had gone to bed, Clara lay in her room reliving all that had happened that evening. She gazed at the ceiling, thinking about the tree and the music and most of all the nutcracker, whose face was so grotesque and yet somehow so brave. She had a sudden longing to see the little man again, so she slipped out of her bed and down the stairs.

The drawing room was dark, but Clara had no trouble picking out the gaily painted face of the nutcracker beneath the Christmas tree. She went over to her new friend, lay down beside him, and fell into a deep sleep.

As the hour approached midnight, there was a noise in the room. Clara awoke and peered into the darkness.

Slinking toward her was a mouse as big as a man. Its eyes were red, and its fur was a dull, matted gray.

Clara rubbed her eyes, then looked again. The mouse had been joined by ten others just like it. They circled around her, drawing closer and closer. When they were near enough to touch, the clock chimed the first stroke of midnight.

Next to her, the nutcracker moved. Yawning and stretching, he climbed to his feet. Then, as the clock kept striking, he began to grow. By the time the twelfth chime died away, he was no longer a small wooden nutcracker. He was Nutcracker, a real-life soldier standing six feet tall.

Clara was thrilled. Nutcracker put one arm around her and drew his sword with the other. The mice backed away.

There was a puff of smoke, and out of it stepped another mouse. Bigger and uglier than the others, it wore a crown and carried a sword, like the mouse in the puppet show. Clara was looking at the evil Mouse King.

Encouraged by the arrival of their leader, the other mice edged forward once again. Nutcracker brandished his sword, but it was clear that he and Clara would soon be surrounded.

When all seemed lost, a bugle sounded from the direction of the Christmas tree. The toy soldiers were stirring! Clara watched in astonishment as they grew to full size and sprang into action.

Under Nutcracker's orders, they fired their cannon and advanced on the mice. A tremendous struggle followed. First one side, then the other, appeared to be winning. The toy soldiers' line heaved forward, and back, and forward again. The room was filled with the sounds of battle.

At the point where the two armies met, Nutcracker and the Mouse King crossed swords. The Mouse King was stronger, but Nutcracker used his quickness and skill to dodge the blows. The two leaders circled, thrusting and parrying, as Clara shouted encouragement from the side.

Then it happened. The Mouse King lunged, and
Nutcracker went down. The giant mouse raised its
arms in triumph and strutted around its fallen vic-
tim.

But Nutcracker was not through. He struggled to his feet, his face contorted in pain, and challenged the Mouse King once again. The ugly gray creature closed in to finish him off.

Perhaps the Mouse King was careless. Perhaps Nutcracker was inspired by Clara's shouts. Or perhaps some greater force was at work, pulling invisible strings.

Whatever the cause, all Clara saw was the flash of Nutcracker's sword and the sudden halt of his opponent. The next thing she knew, the Mouse King lay dead on the floor, and Nutcracker had fallen motionless beside him.

The sounds of battle stopped as fighters from both sides, stunned, dropped their weapons and stepped back. The mice gathered up the body of their leader and carried it off, their steps slow and funereal.

Clara, meanwhile, rushed to the fallen Nutcracker and knelt beside him. She took his hand and smoothed his brow, searching for signs of life. She saw none.

In the silence, there were footsteps. Clara looked up and saw her godfather standing over her.

She threw herself into his arms. "Oh, Godpapa," she cried, "what can I do?"

Her godfather held her close and murmured, "Don't worry, Clara. Godpapa Drosselmeier will fix your dream." He reached down and touched the fallen warrior's shoulder.

Nutcracker's eyes popped open.

Clara gasped, then watched in awe as his face began to change. The bright colors melted together, and the gaping mouth and eyes took on a pleasing shape. Seconds later, Clara was looking at a dashing prince.

"Thank you, Godpapa," she said, hugging the old man tight. "Thank you for saving him."

"Ah, but Clara," he replied, smiling, "it was you who saved him with the power of your love."

"My lady," said a voice from behind Clara. She turned and saw the new, handsome Nutcracker holding out his hand. She took it, and he pulled her close and kissed her. As he did, her nightdress was transformed into a long silk gown, and the air seemed to shimmer.

When she looked up, her godfather and the drawing room were gone, and in their place was a sparkling winter scene. Icicles glistened from tree branches, and snowflakes danced overhead.

Nutcracker snapped his fingers, and across the fields came a sleigh pulled by a team of white horses. It stopped next to them, and Nutcracker helped Clara in.

The prince and his new princess sped across the ice and snow, over hills and gullies and frozen streams. Clara saw a purple banner waving above the trees, and moments later a magnificent castle towered above them.

As they rode through the gates, there were shouts of greeting. Hundreds of people rushed forward with smiling faces and outstretched hands.

The royal couple stepped out of the sleigh and made their way into a vast high-ceilinged hall where an even bigger crowd waited. At one end of the room were two thrones. Nutcracker escorted her to one and placed a crown on her head. The people cheered.

Nutcracker faced the audience. "And now," he said, "let the celebration begin!"

Music rang out, and two Spanish dancers whirled and leaped their way around the floor. They were followed by Chinese dancers, then Russian. And finally, the Sugar Plum Fairy led her fairy court in a lilting waltz around the room. When all had finished, Nutcracker turned to Clara.

"My lady," he said, "this next dance is the best, for it is ours."

He took her into his arms, and the music began. As they circled the floor together, sunbeams shone through a window and bathed the couple in golden light.

Then a shadow passed in front of the window, and an icy wind blew. Out of the corner of her eye, Clara saw Godfather Drosselmeier standing at the edge of the crowd.

The music grew slow and somehow sad. It began to fade, and with it faded the room and the crowd and finally, no matter how tightly she clung to him, Nutcracker himself faded.

Clara found herself back in the drawing room, alone on the floor beside a small wooden nutcracker. Taking the figure in her arms, she went to the front door and peered out into the night.

Snow was falling in the streets of the village, but Clara didn't see it. She was looking beyond to a land of dancers and white horses and a prince whose face glowed with love.